THE WARRIOR'S ROAD

SKURIK
THE FOREST
DEMON

With special thanks to Michael Ford

For Joseph Hutchinson

www.beastquest.co.uk

ORCHARD BOOKS
338 Euston Road, London NW1 3BH
Orchard Books Australia
Level 17/207 Kent St, Sydney, NSW 2000

A Paperback Original
First published in Great Britain in 2013

Beast Quest is a registered trademark of Beast Quest Limited
Series created by Beast Quest Limited, London

Text © Beast Quest Limited 2013
Cover and inside illustrations by Steve Sims © Orchard Books 2013

A CIP catalogue record for this book is available from
the British Library.

ISBN 978 1 40832 402 8

3 5 7 9 10 8 6 4 2

Printed in Great Britain by CPI Group (UK) Ltd, Croydon, CR0 4YY

Orchard Books is a division of Hachette Children's Books,
an Hachette UK company

www.hachette.co.uk

SKURIK
THE FOREST
DEMON

BY ADAM BLADE

ORCHARD

The Warrior's Road

COSHTIN PROVINCE

PYRUS

THE LAST CITY

MARBLE CASTLE

Greetings, whoever reads this.

I am Tanner, Avantia's first Master of the Beasts. I fear I have little time left. My life slips away, and I write these few words as a testament for whoever may come across my remains. I have reached the end of my final journey. But a new warrior's journey is just beginning...

With the death of a Master, a new hero must take on the responsibility of guarding the kingdom of Avantia. Avantia needs a true warrior to wear the Golden Armour. He or she must walk the Warrior's Road – a test of valour and strength. I have succeeded, but it has cost me my life. I only hope those who follow survive.

May fortune be with you,

Tanner

PROLOGUE

Kreg's legs were getting cramped from crouching so long. He straightened up, and looked over the edge of the hollow tree stump. There was no sign of Rik or any of the others.

Kreg wondered how long he'd been there. Perhaps the others had already been found and he'd won the game of hide and seek. He hopped out from his secret place, and brushed dead leaves off his tunic.

"No one ever finds me here," he

muttered under his breath. Through the trees, he could hear the distant sounds of the village fete – pipes and singing and drums. *I bet Rik has gone back to eat the suckling pig*, he thought.

Kreg walked through the forest, retracing his steps towards the village. All Errinel stopped work on this day each year because it was the birthday of Taladon, their greatest hero. Taladon's brother, the village blacksmith Henry, organised huge platters of food and music and dancing long into the night.

The crunch of footsteps made Kreg stop suddenly. He spun around.

"Rik, is that you?"

His voice sounded very small among the looming trees.

Another cracking branch made him turn the other way.

A shadow slipped across the forest floor slowly to his left.

Kreg started to follow it, breaking out into a run. Perhaps it was Rik. He called ahead, but no answering voice came. He was sure he'd seen and heard someone. Kreg walked a little farther from the path he knew. Was someone playing a trick on him?

"Rik!" he called again. *"Rik!"*

Still no answer. Kreg looked around and suddenly realised he was lost. He couldn't hear the music from the village any more.

Kreg felt his heartbeat speed up. *Where am I?* he wondered. He suddenly ached to be home, digging into that delicious pig and watching the older boys and girls dance. A flutter of panic bloomed in his chest and he began to run, hard and fast.

Branches whipped his face, but Kreg pressed on through the dark forest, his breathing ragged. *I'll never play hide and seek again*, he thought. *I'll stay in the village and…*

He skidded on a patch of wet ground and his feet shot from beneath him. He fell heavily on his back, knocking the air from his lungs. But what loomed over him made Kreg shriek in horror.

Above, hanging from the trees, were strange balls of dripping slime. Kreg stared at his hands and realised they were covered with the same strange gloopy substance. He must have grabbed at one as he fell. The gloopy stuff stank like rotten leaf mulch. But wait…inside the balls, *things* were moving.

Kreg's heart thumped against his

ribcage. He managed to scramble to a standing position, his legs trembling.

Inside the blobs of slime, he made out limbs – legs, arms, fingers pressing against the walls to be freed. He saw a head, a face, and realised with terror that it was Rik!

His eyes scanned the other balls.

"Heidi…" he mumbled. And there were Gavin, Lysa and Derren, all his playmates, imprisoned too.

A slick, slithering sound at his back made Kreg spin around. What he faced was such a horror, it took him a while to understand what he was seeing. The creature looked like a giant maggot, a white body pulsating as it moved across the forest floor, leaving a trail of silvery slime. Dozens of beady black eyes were watching him, and between them opened a dark chasm of a mouth. Hundreds of spiked teeth spiralled deep into its throat.

Kreg's hand was shaking, but he managed to draw his wooden sword and hold it aloft. A hiss sounded from the monster's throat, and mucus sprayed into Kreg's face. He dropped the sword and tried to shield himself, but the sickening slime flooded over him. He fell to the ground. Soon it was hard even to move in the gluey, stinking mess. The creature's shadow fell over him.

Screams tore through Kreg's throat, but he knew full well that no one would hear them.

CHAPTER ONE

AN EVIL SUMMONS

Tom stared out over the castle walls from the window of his bedchamber.

"I hate waiting," he said. "We should be *doing* something!"

"What?" said Elenna, behind him. "We can't even find the Judge!"

Tom turned to his friend, who was sitting on a chest, restringing her trusty bow. Silver the wolf lay at her feet, his ears pricked up.

"He could be up to something," said Tom. "Evil never rests."

But what can we do?

He'd sent his sword to be sharpened three times since they'd been back at King Hugo's palace. Its blade could slice through leather with just a weak swing. He practised daily against the finest of the king's knights, to keep himself in top form. Each day he hoped the King would call on him and announce a new Quest to save the kingdom.

"When the Judge comes, we'll be ready," said Elenna.

Tom let out a growl. Even the thought of the Judge made his blood boil. The Circle of Wizards was supposed to be a force for good, but only Tom, Elenna and Avantia's wizard Daltec knew the truth. The Judge, who led the Circle, was corrupt. He'd sided with Kensa the sorceress and Sanpao the Pirate King, promising to bring destruction to Avantia.

Tom remembered how Aduro, his true friend and once a powerful wizard, had been stripped of his magical powers by the Judge. He remained a wise man, but a broken one – old and weak.

"We should tell King Hugo what we've learned," said Elenna. "He needs to know that the Judge is no friend and the Circle of Wizards cannot be trusted."

Tom had thought about it, but there was no point in worrying the king. "King Hugo can't do anything," he said. "The Circle of Wizards exists in a magical realm where the King has no power."

His words died as the walls around him seemed to shimmer. Colours blurred as if he were seeing the chamber through a waterfall. Silver yapped in panic.

"We're being summoned," whispered Elenna.

A sudden wind gusted around Tom from every direction at once, whipping at his clothes.

At last! thought Tom. *A Quest!*

WHOOSH!

The room vanished, but instead of finding himself in King Hugo's throne room, Tom saw they were standing in the circular Wizards' Courtroom, the place where Aduro had been punished so cruelly. Elenna appeared at his side, and also Daltec, dressed in a red robe. Tom nodded to his friend, whose face was pale and grim.

"Thank you for joining us," said a sinister voice.

Tom looked up. On a high bench sat the Judge and around each side, on curved seats, were the rest of the Circle of Wizards, all wearing robes of different colours. Tom felt a dark thrill at the sight of his old enemy.

"We had no choice," said Elenna. "What do you want?"

The Judge raised his eyebrows. "Why are you being so grumpy?" he asked. "We brought you here to congratulate you on your last Quest. The Lightning Beasts are vanquished."

Tom's grip tightened on his sword. He wondered if he could get close enough to the Judge to deliver a fatal blow.

"Oh, you won't be needing that," said the Judge, clicking his fingers.

Tom found himself grasping thin air. His sword had vanished! Grim-faced, Tom turned to his enemy.

"Do your fellow wizards know the truth about you?" Tom said. *If I tell them he's working with Sanpao and*

Kensa, they're sure to overthrow him.

The Judge waved a hand, and crystal goblets studded with jewels appeared in front of all the wizards.

They lifted them and murmurs of pleasure filled the room.

"First, a toast," said the Judge, raising his own cup. "To Tom's triumph."

"To Tom's triumph!" shouted the wizards, all taking sips of their drinks.

Tom felt his stomach twist. "This charade makes me sick," he said, pointing at the Judge. "Hear me, esteemed Wizards! Your leader is a traitor. He fights alongside your enemies and…"

Elenna seized Tom's arm. "Look, Tom! The wizards!"

Tom stared around the room and gasped. Each wizard was perfectly still. Some held goblets to their lips, others stared blankly into the chamber.

"What have you done to them?"

asked Daltec. He raised his hands and muttered a spell. Green light shone from his palms, and he levelled them at the Judge. A bolt of emerald shot towards the high bench, but the Judge merely lifted a finger. Daltec's bolt of light seemed to bounce off it, and smashed back into the young wizard's chest. Daltec cried out as his body slammed into a column.

He sank to the floor without a sound, and lay there motionless.

CHAPTER TWO

THE WARRIOR'S ROAD

Elenna ran to Daltec's side, cradling his body. Tom saw that Aduro's apprentice was bleeding from a cut on his head.

"Is he...dead?" Tom asked, aghast.

"He'll live," said the Judge. "The young boy has courage, but he is a fool. I've more power than he can ever dream of."

"And Daltec has more honour than *you* can dream of," said Elenna.

The Judge snarled and turned his attention to Tom.

"You didn't really think I'd let you tell my secrets, did you? Now, would you like to know why I really brought you here?"

He held one palm in the air, and muttered a spell. Sparks flickered

over his fingers and a roll of parchment took shape before Tom's eyes. "This is the Warlock's Scroll," he said. "Take a look."

He let go of the Scroll and it floated through the air, down towards Tom. Tom took it and unrolled it carefully. Instead of paper, the Scroll was made of some sort of animal hide – smooth to the touch and so cold it made him shiver. He read the pale brown script aloud:

"*On this day, in the one hundred and ninetieth year after Tanner, we, the Circle of Wizards, do hereby outlaw the Master's Trial. Henceforth no Warrior shall walk the Road…*"

"Tanner?" said Elenna. "Wasn't he the first Master of the Beasts?"

"Yes," said Tom. He recalled seeing Tanner's burial place in the Gallery of Tombs. Tom had fought Mortaxe, the Skeleton Warrior, who Tanner had once vanquished too. "What's the Trial?" he asked.

Daltec shuffled on the ground and managed to sit up weakly.

"The Master's Trial is an ancient practice," he said. "It was once used to decide who would become the new Master or Mistress of the Beasts. But so few candidates survived, it was decided that the Trial should be banned."

The Judge clapped slowly. "You know your history better than your spells, boy," he said. A smile crept over his lips. "Only seven survived, and hundreds perished. The Warlock's Scroll is there to protect lives." He clicked his fingers again. In Tom's hand, the Scroll blackened in its

centre, then caught fire. Orange
flames crept over the surface and
Tom dropped it to the ground. In
no time at all, the Scroll was just
crumbling grey flakes of ash.

"That's forbidden!" cried Daltec.
"The Scroll is law!"

"Not any more," said the Judge.

Tom frowned. "I don't understand."

The Judge smirked. "Don't you? Well, let me make it clear. You will undertake the Trial, Tom. Perhaps you will be the eighth to live, but more likely you will join the long list of the dead."

"No!" said Elenna. "That's not fair."

Tom felt a cold dread as he looked at the remains of the Scroll. *I was waiting for a Quest, and here it is – the most dangerous Quest of all.*

"It's all right," he told Elenna. "I'll tackle the Trial and I will triumph."

"Brave words," said the Judge, "but there's one more thing…"

Tom felt suddenly unsure of himself, as if his strength was draining away through his feet. He felt dizzy and staggered sideways.

"What's happening?" he asked,

steadying himself.

The Judge cackled. "You've relied on the Golden Armour too long," he said. "I've stripped its powers from you."

"You have no right!" cried Tom. "I'm Master of the Beasts – the Golden Armour is mine!"

"Not any more," said the Judge. "Until you complete the Trial, Avantia *has* no Master of the Beasts. You're just a boy with dreams of glory, like all the others who failed before you."

Tom's rage burned brighter than ever and he reached for the hilt of his sword. He felt like launching himself at the Judge, then and there, but a flurry of doubts stopped him.

Of course! The Judge has taken the Golden Breastplate. He's sapped my strength of heart…

"Why should I trust you?" Tom asked.

The Judge grinned. "I didn't say you should. But refuse this Quest and Avantia has no rightful Master of the Beasts. The whole kingdom will be at the mercy of Evil."

Tom took in the stony faces of the

other Wizards, then the mocking features of the Judge. *He has complete control*, he thought. *We're powerless against him, unless I can complete the Trial.*

"Tell me more," he said, gritting his teeth.

"No, Tom!" said Elenna. "He's just trying to trick you, to see you killed."

"He won't succeed," said Tom grimly.

The Judge rubbed his hands together. "You must walk the Warrior's Road," he said. "An ancient path from Tanner's resting place in the Gallery of Tombs to the site of his final battle. Only then will you prove yourself a worthy Master of the Beasts. Until that time, you are a fraud, just like your father."

Tom's face burned. *How dare he*

insult my father's memory! He longed to wrap his hands around the Judge's throat and wring the life from him. *But I wouldn't even get close*. The only way to defeat the Judge was to take on the Trial. *And until I do, Avantia is vulnerable*.

"Please," begged Daltec. "It's been over two hundred years since a Master of the Beasts was made to walk the Road. The danger is too great. Tom will be killed."

The Judge sat back on his seat, his lips curling with cruelty.

"So be it," he said. "If Tom wants to be Avantia's champion, he must earn it. Of course, if he wants to slink away like a coward..."

Never! thought Tom.

"I'll do it," shouted Tom. "While there's blood in my veins, I'll walk the Warrior's Road!"

For Avantia, and for my father's memory.

CHAPTER THREE

FIRST STEPS ON THE WARRIOR'S ROAD

"This is a Quest too far," said King Hugo. "I can't allow it."

Tom and Elenna stood with Aduro and the King in the throne room. Tom had explained everything that had taken place in the Court of the Wizards, and with each detail King Hugo had looked more worried.

"There's no choice," said Tom. "If I don't walk the Road, the Judge will spread more evil in Avantia."

"And without a Master of the Beasts, the kingdom will be vulnerable," said Elenna.

"Perhaps the King is right," said Aduro, bent over with age, his pale eyes watery. "You've defended this kingdom from countless Beasts, Tom. No one will judge you if you decide it's time to stop. We can send out word across Avantia, asking for new champions who might be able to tackle—"

"No!" said Tom. "This is my Quest. I demand the right to take it on."

"And I won't leave Tom's side," said Elenna.

Her words gave Tom more determination than ever. He shot his friend a grateful smile.

King Hugo and Aduro shared a long look. The King sighed and, at last, nodded.

"Very well," said Aduro. He looked towards the door. "Now, where's Daltec got to?"

The door burst open, and Daltec stumbled in, carrying a mahogany

chest in his arms. A bandage covered the cut on his head where the Judge's blow had struck him.

"Is this the one?" he called. "It was right at the back of the vaults!"

"That's it," said Aduro. "Set it down here."

Daltec let the chest thump to the ground at their feet. The dark wood was carved with symbols like shields and axes, trees and stars. The whole thing was covered with a thick layer of dust.

"I had to delve far back in my records to learn about this chest," said Aduro. "It's been in the vaults for two centuries."

"What's inside?" said Daltec, eyes wide with wonder.

"Let's see, shall we?" Aduro clicked his fingers and nothing happened.

Tom saw sadness mist his eyes. "Old habits," he muttered. "Daltec, perhaps you could help?"

The young wizard nodded, closed his eyes and moved his lips in a spell. The lid slowly opened.

Inside was a single folded piece of parchment. Daltec took it out, then handed it to his master. "This is the last map ever used by a warrior undertaking the Trial," Aduro said.

Tom's throat went dry when he saw the brown stains that marked the parchment. *They look like dried blood...* He peered closer, and frowned at the strange details of the map.

In the bottom left corner he recognised Avantia's capital city. A red line left the city gates and snaked towards the woods beside Tom's home village of Errinel. But from there the map made no sense. Instead of continuing into the Forbidden Lands, there was a huge area of new terrain – a snowy landscape. Beyond that he saw jungle, mountains, a vast sea…

"Avantia must have changed a lot in two hundred years," he said.

Aduro shook his head. "The Trial is not confined to Avantia," he said. "It takes the walker into kingdoms unreachable by normal means. The warrior must follow where the Road leads."

Tom gazed at the map, his eyes travelling over the strange lands. His heart thumped in his chest.

"Is there anything else I need to know?" asked Tom.

Aduro's face darkened. "There will be Beasts," he said. "More terrible than any you have yet faced. Six

Beasts guard the Road, and each tests the warrior who walks it. While the Road is quiet, they sleep, but when they are awoken, so is their anger. But I can tell you no more. Those who walk the Road are sworn never to reveal the nature of the Beasts."

"I'll deal with them as I deal with all the Beasts," said Tom, letting his hand rest on the hilt of his sword. It had magically reappeared when the Judge returned them to Tom's chamber. *At least I'm allowed my weapon*, he thought.

"And I'll be at his side," said Elenna.

Tom stared at his friend. "I can't ask you to join me this time," he said. "The Judge wants to test me alone."

"Who said I need to be asked?" said Elenna, smiling. "This Trial can't be any more dangerous than going to

Henkrall. Or Gorgonia. Or Kayonia. You can't get rid of me that easily!"

Tom grinned. "We should leave at once. The Warrior's Road awaits. I'll saddle Storm and make for Errinel."

Aduro folded the map again. "I'm afraid Storm must stay here," he said. "The Warrior's Road must be walked."

"What about Silver?" Elenna asked.

"It's very dangerous," said Aduro. "If he goes with you, he might not live."

Elenna nodded, and bit her lip. *Even if she wants to leave him behind, Silver won't let her*, thought Tom.

"I don't understand," said the King. "What lies at the end of the Road?"

"I've heard tell of the ultimate Beast," said Aduro. "But I know no more than that."

Tom slid the map inside his tunic, dread and excitement making his stomach squirm.

"Good luck," said King Hugo. "If anyone can succeed on the Warrior's Road, it's you, Tom."

Tom bowed to the King, trying not to notice the doubt in Aduro's eyes.

I'll complete this Quest, he thought. *I have to.*

CHAPTER FOUR

A NASTY HOMECOMING

"I'll miss you, old friend," said Tom, "but this is one Quest you can't come on."

Storm lowered his sleek black head, and nuzzled Tom's shoulder. His eyes were full of understanding.

"He deserves a rest," said Elenna.

As they left the stables, Tom set his mind on the task ahead. *Six Beasts lie between me and this secret. I will not fail.*

"There's one more thing I need to do," said Tom to Elenna. "I'll catch you up at the city gates."

Tom went down some steps behind the kitchen, then followed a set of passages deep beneath the palace. He came to a heavy door, locked tight. Thankfully, Aduro had given him a key. A cold blast of air escaped as Tom

opened the door. He found himself in a dark and damp chamber. As soon as he closed the door behind him, candles lit up magically around the walls, and their flickering light threw shadows among the statues of warriors and carved reliefs of ancient battles.

"The Gallery of Tombs," whispered Tom. He passed the tomb of Tanner, first Master of the Beasts, and that of Mortaxe, the Beast he had defeated. But it wasn't their burial places he was interested in. At the back of the chamber was the newest marble tomb. On its lid lay the statue of a man, clutching his sword across his chest. The name 'TALADON' was inscribed on the side, with the date of his death.

Tom laid his hand on the side of the tomb and kneeled. If this was the Quest that finally killed him, he wanted to say goodbye. *I'm doing this for Avantia*, he thought, *and for my family's honour.*

"Father," he said, "may your strength be with me."

The stone felt warm beneath his touch, and Tom wondered if his father's ghost had heard him. It gave him hope to be here – no one could take away Taladon's achievements, not even the Judge. *And he won't stop me, either*, Tom thought.

Elenna and Silver were waiting for him just beyond the city walls. The grey wolf cocked his head as Tom approached.

"He's wondering where Storm is," said Elenna. Crouching beside Silver, she tickled his neck. "Not this time, brave friend," she said. "It's just the three of us."

Tom checked his map, and saw that the red line led off through the fields rather than on the well-worn track.

"It's this way," he said, pointing through the long grasses.

Sure enough, they soon came upon a wide red track among the grass. It seemed to glow brightly, and swirls of sparkling dust floated over its surface like dancing cinders from a bonfire. *Strange*, Tom thought, *I never even knew this was here!* He pressed on ahead, and his mind turned once again to the Judge's hateful face.

I'll prove my worth, he thought. *And when I've reached the end of the Road, I'll deal with you too.*

"Are you sure you know where you're going?" said Elenna. "That map might not be reliable after so long."

Tom paused and looked back. His friend was veering off into the grass.

"I'm just following the path," said Tom. "Where are you going?"

"What path?" she said.

Tom frowned. "This one," he said, pointing to the ground.

Elenna's brow furrowed. "There isn't a path there," she said. "It's just grass."

Realisation dawned on Tom. "Only I can see the Road," he muttered. "You'd better follow me."

Elenna grinned. "As long as you leave some of the Beast-fighting to me!"

They reached Errinel late in the afternoon on the third day of hard walking. They'd slept in the shelter of walls at night, or under hedgerows.

With Storm, the journey would have taken less than a day, and Tom had never been so glad to see his home village.

But something was wrong. Tom scanned the sky and saw no trails of smoke from the chimneys. Even when they neared the outskirts of the village there wasn't a sound.

He quickened his steps, towards his uncle's house.

"Come on!" he said to Elenna, drawing his sword.

When they reached it, Tom could see that the house's shutters were barred and the forge was empty. The great furnace had gone out, leaving only ashes in the hearth. Cold dread swept over Tom's body. *What happened here?*

"Uncle Henry!" he called. "Aunt Maria?" There was no answer but the creaking of the blacksmith's sign hanging over the forge door.

They walked on into the central square of Errinel. Here too doors were locked, and windows shuttered up. Trestle tables, some knocked over, filled one side of the square, covered with rotten food and half-empty platters. Toppled flagons stained the ground with spilt drink. Bunting strung between the buildings fluttered gently, but some had been torn down and trailed in the dirt. A cart lay on its side, its wheels smashed. Silver sniffed uncertainly at a roast chicken that had fallen into the embers of the cook-fire.

"They were celebrating," muttered Elenna. "Something must have attacked them."

Among the debris, Tom found a trail of slime, like those left by slugs, but six paces wide. It led out of the village towards the forest. He crouched down and touched the gluey substance then brought his fingers to his nose. He almost gagged with the foul stench. "A Beast," he said. "That's the only thing that could have done this."

Then he saw his father.

Startled, Tom stood up, but quickly realised what he was seeing. A life-size portrait of his father, wearing the Golden Armour, leaned up against the door to the village hall.

"Of course!" he said. "It was Taladon's birthday yesterday. We celebrate it every year in Errinel."

A knocking sound came from across the square and Tom drew his sword.

The Beast might still be here.

Then he heard what sounded like a moan. It was coming from the tavern, a two-storey timber building. Tom saw one wall had collapsed and the roof leaned in at an awkward angle. Elenna crept beside him, an arrow at the ready on her bowstring. There were more trails of slime all around the walls.

Tom stepped foward. At the wooden door, he put a finger to his lips. Silver's hackles were up, his teeth bared.

Tom pushed open the door. Behind it, under an upturned table, were Aunt Maria and Uncle Henry, quaking with fear. His uncle was clutching a chair leg like a weapon. When she saw Tom, his aunt's eyes went wide.

"Tom?" she said. "Oh, Tom, it's you!"

Tom sheathed his sword.

"Nephew!" said his uncle, dropping the chair leg. "I can't believe it!"

They crept out from beneath the table, wearing happy smiles.

As they did, a roof timber groaned above. Then a huge beam separated from the gable, shifting with a splintering sound.

Elenna screamed. "It's going to collapse!"

Then the beam fell inwards, plunging towards his aunt and uncle.

CHAPTER FIVE

THE LOST CHILDREN OF ERRINEL

Tom sprang forward, shield raised, and the beam crunched onto its surface, almost knocking Tom to his knees.

"Quickly!" he said with a grimace. "Get out while you can!"

Elenna bravely entered the tavern and tugged his aunt and uncle towards the door. Tom watched them crawl to safety as debris rained down. With the strength of the Golden Breastplate, Tom knew he would have been fine. But without it, he could barely stay on his feet under the crushing weight of the beam. Sections of the roof crashed into the tavern around him, smashing bottles and chairs. Roof tiles exploded into shards as they hit the ground.

"You have to get out or you'll be crushed!" yelled Elenna from the doorway. Tom gritted his teeth and strained. *If I move, the whole thing will collapse...but I can't fail now, not before I've even faced the first Beast!*

Elenna's words fired Tom's courage. He took a deep breath, and shoved upwards as hard as he could, giving himself a tiny moment. He dived for the door, rolling through it, just as the roof crashed down into the tavern.

A cloud of dust and splinters burst from the doorway and Tom picked himself up outside.

Aunt Maria gripped him in a tight embrace and Uncle Henry clapped him on the back. "You saved our lives, nephew," he said. "Thank you."

Tom managed to free himself, and straightened his filthy tunic. "What happened here?" he asked.

His uncle and aunt shared a terrified look, then his aunt spoke, glancing around the square in dismay. "It was the day of Taladon's feast," she said. "We were celebrating like we always do. There was music, dancing, singing. Round Olly was doing his juggling, but then we noticed the children had not come back from their games in the forest. We sent out search parties, and only one man returned, wild-eyed and

saying something about a 'forest demon'
snatching our young ones. Many
villagers fled, but we hid ourselves in
the tavern. Then the Beast came!"

She began to weep, and Tom's Uncle
Henry put his arm around her shoulder
and continued the tale. "I didn't get a
good look," he said, "but I did manage to
glimpse its pale flesh, all squirming and
wrinkled." He pointed to the toppled

cart. "Bigger than that wagon, it was. And it smelled like rotting food. Some sort of slug, searching for prey among the remains of our feast. It must have sniffed us out, because it battered the tavern walls until dusk. Thank goodness it couldn't get inside – I don't know what we would have done."

Tom nodded at his uncle and took Elenna aside. "This is my fault," he whispered. "The Beast has appeared because I agreed to walk the Warrior's Road. Isn't this what Aduro said would happen?" He turned to his aunt and uncle. "I'll find the children and deal with this Beast. You must go back to your forge. Take Silver to guard you."

Aunt Maria looked at the wolf fearfully. "Is he tame?" she asked.

Elenna smiled. "He knows his friends," she said. "If you have a bone or two, all the better."

Silver whined as they left, but Elenna pointed to Henry and Maria. "Keep them safe, boy. We'll return soon."

On the outskirts of the village, Tom spotted the sparkling red track again, leading past a well and towards the trees. "This way," he said to Elenna.

What sort of Beast steals children? Tom wondered. And why had it attacked his village? Surely it only wanted *him*.

At the edge of the forest, Elenna paused. "Did you hear something?"

"No," said Tom. But then he heard footsteps, coming through the trees.

Tom and Elenna ducked beside a tree stump, and Tom slowly drew his sword.

With the footsteps came the sound of low voices, too indistinct to make out. Tom felt his muscles relax. "It's just people," he said, standing up cautiously.

Tom could see desperate faces lit by
torches. A group of men and women
carried makeshift weapons – a hoe, a
poker and the iron tip of a plough. The
head of the band pointed a rusty sword
at Tom and Elenna.

"The child-snatchers!" he cried
angrily. "Kill them!"

CHAPTER SIX

A DEADLY DEAL

Tom ducked as the man swung his rusty sword. He gave the man a swipe across the thigh with the flat of his blade, enough to make him drop to the ground with a cry. The rest of the band surged past their fallen leader and attacked. Tom felt a blow to his shoulder that sent him staggering sideways, and an arc of flame from a torch backed him up against a tree.

Elenna, without time to nock an arrow, was swinging her bow like a staff, keeping the attackers at bay.

"Stop!" yelled Tom, as he avoided a stab from a woman with a poker. "I don't want to fight you!"

With a twist of his blade, the poker went spinning from the woman's hand. He shoved another man in the chest with his shield. The man tripped, dropped his club, and sprawled on the ground, groaning.

Elenna rapped a shaven-headed man across the knuckles with her bow and he let go of his staff with a cry.

"Why, you little..." he began to say, but his words dried up when he saw that the rest of the band had backed away. They looked at one another, as if daring one of their number to lead the attack. But none was willing to take

Tom and Elenna on. Tom recognised
the bald man as Erik, Errinel's butcher.
And the woman who'd almost
plunged a poker in his belly was the
seamstress, Gara.

"That's enough," said Tom, breathing
heavily. "Don't you know me? It's
Tom, son of Taladon."

A murmur went through the villagers, and a rake-thin man stepped forward. It was Lennard, the carpenter. He held a torch closer to Tom and squinted.

"Tom?" he said. "Is it really you?"

Tom sheathed his sword. "Yes. And this is my friend, Elenna."

Elenna looped her bow back over her shoulder.

"Tom," said Gara, dropping to her knees at his feet. "We're so sorry! If we'd known… I fear that our grief has driven us half mad."

"Grief?" said Tom. "What happened here?"

"I'm sorry, but you're too late," said Gara. "The Forest Demon has already taken our little ones."

"All of them?" Tom asked.

Gara nodded. "It came to the village,

and there was nothing we could do. Oh, Tom, it was horrible, like some sort of giant maggot – unstoppable." She lowered her head. "I'm afraid to say that many of us ran."

"But now, we mean to hunt it down," said Lennard. "Whatever it takes to get our children back and bring vengeance to this creature, we will do it."

Tom laid his hands on Gara's shoulders and helped her to her feet. He turned to speak to them all, looking at each face in turn.

"You all know something many others do not. You know who I really am, who my father was before me."

"Master of the Beasts," whispered Erik in wide-eyed awe.

Tom nodded. "I've been fighting Beasts since the day I left Errinel," said

Tom. "Let me fight this one too."

Lennard's face hardened in the orange glow of the torchlight. "It took my boy. It took Kreg."

"And my daughter Heidi," the butcher added.

The other villagers spoke up too, each saying the name of one they'd lost. Tom could hear their fear and anguish.

"Let's kill the demon!" roared Lennard, waving his torch towards the forest. "Let's burn it!"

"No!" said Elenna, stepping forward. "Fire is not the answer here. You'll burn the whole forest down."

"If that's what we need to do," said Lennard, "so be it."

The villagers lifted their torches and cried out in agreement.

Tom held up a hand. "This forest Beast came on my father's feast day," he said. "In the name of Taladon, let me take it on. Let me rescue your children."

Lennard lowered his torch with a frown, and looked to the other villagers.

"Perhaps he's right," said Gara.

"But what if he fails?" said Erik.

"I've never failed before," said Tom. But he knew this would be his most difficult Quest of all. *I can only hope I don't fail now.*

Lennard turned to Tom, and his eyes glistened in the torchlight. "Very well, Tom," he said. "You have until dusk. Find our children and punish this demon who took them. If at sunset you haven't returned, we will have no choice – the forest, and everything in it, will burn."

"Thank you," said Tom. "I swear I won't let you down."

Lennard and the villagers began to make their way back towards Errinel, and soon their torches were distant flickers.

"Are you sure about this?" asked Elenna.

Tom felt a tingle of dread in his heart. "I made a promise," he said. "And while there's blood in my veins, I'll keep it." He took out the map of the Warrior's Road.

Sure enough, the route seemed to lead
further into the depths of the trees.

Looking up, Tom saw the glittering
red path trailing over the mossy
ground. *Odd*, he thought. *Sometimes I
see it, but sometimes I don't.*

He turned to Elenna. "Let's hunt
down this Forest Demon!" he said.

CHAPTER SEVEN

A STICKY SITUATION

Tom had always loved the forest as a child. When he wasn't helping in his uncle's forge, he'd spent whole days climbing trees or building forts from fallen branches. He'd carved his own wooden swords, and slashed at the tree trunks, pretending to be a great warrior.

Now he was here facing a real

enemy, with a real blade at his hip.
The trees pressed closer around them
as they pushed on towards the centre
of the forest. Branches seemed to
reach out and stroke their faces, and
every little sound set Tom's nerves
tingling. He wished they'd brought
Silver with them.

"Are we still following the Warrior's Road?" hissed Elenna.

Tom nodded. The red track led over strewn leaves and gnarled roots, and at one point right through a tree, emerging on the other side. Tom walked around the huge trunk. *It's an ancient path, forged when this forest was just saplings*, he thought. *Tanner walked this route once, four hundred years ago. I wonder what Avantia looked like then.*

Tom's nostrils twitched at an unusual smell – the same slightly rotten stink that hung over Errinel's market square. "The Beast is near," he said.

Elenna wafted a hand in front of her nose. "At least it can't sneak up on us."

The stench grew even stronger as they walked on. Soon it was making Tom's stomach turn over, and he fought against the urge to retch.

Elenna's eyes were watering.

They came across the source of the smell – a silvery track like the one back in the village, but this one was glistening and fresh. The vegetation beneath was slowly turning black and rotten.

Tom pulled his tunic up over his nose. "We need to follow this trail," he said.

Elenna wrinkled her nose, and pulled up her tunic too.

The slimy path took them away from the Warrior's Road, and it wasn't long before Tom began to lose his bearings. All the trees looked the same. *Which way is Errinel now?*

"Maybe we should stick to the Warrior's Road," said Elenna. "If we get lost, you can't complete your Quest."

"What about the children?" said

Tom. "The Beast must have brought them this way."

"But what if the Beast is just trying to distract you?" she said.

Tom paused for a moment. *She might be right, but what choice do I have?* "I'm willing to take that risk," he said eventually. "I can't let innocent children die, Quest or not."

He drew his sword and let his shield drop from his shoulder onto his forearm. If the Beast attacked, he'd be ready. His magical tokens gave him the power to resist fire and extreme cold. *It's a shame there isn't one to protect me against foul smells too!*

A distant cry reached his ears and he stopped dead. Elenna walked into the back of him.

"What is it?" she asked.

"Listen!" Tom whispered.

For a moment, there was no sound, then it came again – a desperate call. A child's cry!

"The children!" Tom said, pointing to their left. "This way!"

He quickened his steps, breaking into a run between the trees. The cries grew louder. Closer. He heard Elenna's steps, right on his heels. Tom adjusted his direction, sprinting now, gripping his sword hilt tightly.

"Tom, wait!" said Elenna.

But Tom was desperate to find the children. The sounds seemed to fade, so he changed his path again, towards them. The cries were louder once more – he thought he could hear at least three separate voices, but all were indistinct.

Tom tripped over a root, but kept running. Branches lashed his face. *If the children are still alive, there is hope…*

He paused to catch his breath and realised the sounds no longer came from right ahead. They seemed to echo from at least three sides, mingling with the wind in the leaves.

"You may be right," he said to Elenna. "The Beast might be playing a trick."

Elenna didn't reply. Tom turned, and saw he was alone.

"Elenna?" he said.

No answer.

Tom could hear the children's desperate calls. Their voices were muffled, as though they had gags over their mouths. But he had to find Elenna!

He began to retrace his steps through the forest.

He soon heard a new sound. *Elenna!*

Tom followed the sound, running through long grasses that whipped at his thighs. He found her between two trees, struggling to free herself from a pool of the pale slime. It seemed to be snaking up her shins and legs like strands of a spider's web. She clutched a low branch with her hands, and tried to heave herself upwards. "Tom!" she said. "I was trying to keep up, but I lost you. Help me!"

As she spoke, one of the strands of slime reached up over her waist and wrapped itself around her chest. Another snaked up towards her throat. Tom saw the slime stiffen around her like a cage.

"Don't panic," said Tom. "Hold still."

Carefully he slipped his blade under the hardening tendrils and cut them

free. But others grew up to take their place. It was as if the goo had a mind of its own, intent on swallowing up his friend. One strand latched onto her arm and fixed it to her side, so

she could only grip the branch above
with one hand. Tom sliced through
the strand and his blade glistened.
He fought not to gag at the horrible
stench. One of the tendrils found
his arm, but Tom snatched it quickly
away. Elenna's feet were sinking
deeper into the horrible pale sludge.

"You'll have to step out of your
boots," said Tom.

"Cut the laces!" said Elenna.
"Quickly!"

Tom crouched beside her, not
daring to get too close in case the
slime reached for his face and he
could never tear free. He slid his
sword tip under Elenna's laces and
cut one set. He was about to do the
same with the other boot, when he
heard a sound that chilled his blood.
A slick slithering like a wet mouth

opening, filled with drool.

At his waist, the ruby in his belt glowed, and a wave of evil intent swept over Tom's chest and clutched his heart like a cold fist. He'd won the ruby from Torgor the Minotaur and it gave him the power to hear the thoughts of the Beasts. He sensed a voice calling to him:

Skurik is here, Walker of the Road. Prepare to meet your end...

CHAPTER EIGHT

PRISONS OF SLIME

Tom sliced through the laces of Elenna's other boot and she pulled herself nimbly up to the branch above, then swung herself over the slime to Tom's side.

"Skurik is close," said Tom. "He sent me a message."

"Is that the name of the Beast?" asked Elenna.

Tom tapped the ruby at his belt so

she would understand. "Our first foe on the Warrior's Road," he said.

A grey shape, like a smoky ghost, passed between the trees in the distance. A terrible stink filled Tom's nose. As the Beast emerged through the darkness, Tom couldn't help shuddering. Even his uncle's description of the Beast hadn't prepared him for such a repulsive sight.

Skurik was like a giant pale slug, his body rippling with muscles that contracted and stretched as his bulk shifted over the undergrowth. It seemed half melted, like dripping and congealed tree sap. Dozens of eyes glinted from his head, and his mouth was a lipless puckered hole in the centre of his face. As he pushed through the trees towards them,

the smell was worse than anything
Tom had ever experienced. Each
breath brought a wave of dizziness
that threatened to weaken his knees.
Elenna's hand was covering her
mouth.

*I don't know if I can even stand, let
alone fight!* he thought.

Skurik spied them, and his black
eyes sparkled. His mouth stretched
open, a gaping maw filled with teeth
like glass splinters. Strings of drool

stretched between them and it hissed in anger. Tom dreaded to think if any children had been taken by those terrible jaws.

"Be careful!" said Tom.

Elenna strung two arrows and loosed them towards Skurik. Both found their targets, sinking into the Beast's soft flank. But the Beast barely slowed, and the arrows slipped out of his hide with a squelching noise.

Tom doubted whether his sword's blade would have any more effect. He pointed to the tree beside them. "We should climb up. Skurik won't be able to follow and we can form a plan."

Elenna went first, shinning up the tree trunk. The Beast made a sudden surge between the trees towards Tom, moving faster than he could have imagined possible. Skurik's mouth gaped wider with a choking sound, as though he was clearing his throat. Tom leaped up to the lowest branch and pulled his legs clear as a blast of sludge shot from the Forest Demon's mouth, splatting into the tree trunk. *So that's where the slime comes from.* Another sticky blast followed as Tom climbed out of reach. Elenna waited for him on a high branch.

"What now?"

Tom scanned the tree-tops, and saw them thinning out a short distance to his left. "There's a clearing!" he said. "If we can lure Skurik there, maybe we can tackle him on open ground."

With Elenna at his side, Tom clambered along the branch as far as he dared, then leaped to the next tree. The branch he landed on creaked and bent, but held. Below,

Skurik roared and hissed, and vomited forth another mouthful of slime. It coated the leaves below, but didn't reach Tom's feet. *We can't stay up here forever*, he thought. *Sooner or later we'll have to face the Beast.*

They picked their way from tree to tree, placing their feet and hands with care. To fall now would mean a broken leg and certain death in a foul-smelling, sharp-toothed mouth. Skurik trailed through the trunks below, eyes watching for any chance to strike. Tom's fear was growing. Not for himself, but for the children of Errinel. *What has the forest demon done with them?*

Tom was almost at the clearing when Elenna gripped his arm. He rocked on the high branch, but managed to keep his balance.

"Look!" said his friend, pointing through the trees.

Tom gasped. From the branches at the clearing's edge hung at least a dozen pale slimy sacs. They looked like giant seed-pods, suspended from strands of Skurik's spit. Some were wriggling, and through the slimy walls Tom saw bodies squirming to get free. He could hear the muffled cries more clearly now.

"The children!" he said. "They're alive!"

"We need to free them!" said Elenna.

Then a small darting shape caught Tom's eyes. It was crouching beside a tree at the far side of the clearing. *A little girl!* Tom realised it was Sara, the red-headed young daughter of Errinel's master mason.

She was staring up into the trees, fear painted over her dirt-smeared face and leaves caught in her hair. Tom looked down and saw Skurik emerging into the clearing and racing towards her hiding place.

"He's seen her!" said Elenna.

Tom cupped his hand to mouth and yelled to the girl. "Run for your life, Sara!"

The girl looked up, searching for his voice.

"Run away!" Tom cried.

It was too late. A bolt of slime shot from Skurik's mouth, and knocked Sara off her feet. Tom watched in horror as the strands wrapped themselves over her mouth and head. She squirmed on the ground, clawing at the leaves, but it was no use. The drool crept over her limbs, encasing

her completely. Tendrils reached up, found a branch above, and hoisted the writhing sac upwards to hang beside the others.

Tom felt anger blossom in his heart. *Another child sacrificed.*

CHAPTER NINE

FACING THE FOREST DEMON

Tom started to climb down from the tree.

"What are you doing?" asked Elenna, gripping his shoulder.

"I can't sit back and watch!" said Tom. "I've got to…"

His words trailed off as a new smell reached his nose. Not Skurik's foul stink this time, but something else – smoke.

"Dusk is here," said Elenna. "We've

run out of time."

Tom could still see a few rays of sunlight coming through the trees. "No!" he said. "It's too soon!"

If the villagers come into the forest with their torches, we could all burn to death! It was time to end this.

"Do what you can to free the children," he said to Elenna, scrambling down the tree.

He hit the forest floor with barely a sound, but it was enough to alert the Forest Demon. Skurik turned on the spot, his many eyes glistening, and let fly with a mouthful of slime. Tom rolled through the leaves as sludge dripped from the trunk where he'd been standing. A moment later, and he'd have been trapped there.

He broke into a run, and heard the snapping of branches as the Beast pursued him. Skurik snuffled like a hog, his mouth making awful sucking sounds. Tom dared not look back, and leaped to avoid the silvery tracks left on the ground from when the Beast had first entered the forest.

Soon he saw the glow of torches through the trees. The villagers had come to flush the Beast out with fire!

Perhaps Skurik had seen them too, because the sounds of the Beast grew faint. Tom glanced over his shoulder and saw no sign of the Forest Demon. *He must have retreated...*

"Tom! You're alive!"

Tom staggered to a halt as he came face to face with the villagers, creeping through the forest. Each one of them clutched a flaming torch. Gara smiled, looking relieved to see him.

Is Skurik afraid of fire? Tom thought.

Why else would he retreat?

"Out of our way, Tom," said Lennard. "The Beast's fate is in our hands now."

Tom looked up at the fading light. "You're early," he said. "It's not yet dusk."

"We will have our revenge," said the man. "The Forest Demon will burn!"

"Wait!" said Tom. "Your children are alive! I've seen them. We can free them, and there'll be no reason to burn the forest. Let me deal with the Beast."

Lennard was silent for long while. Finally he held out his torch to Tom. "Very well. We trust you, son of Taladon. But don't let us down."

Tom took a single torch and ran back towards the clearing, using the flames to light his way. In the gloom, Skurik's trail glittered like silver. The Beast had turned back from his pursuit. *Back towards Elenna and the children…*

Tom kept the torch low. The last thing he wanted was to start a forest fire, but if he was right – if Skurik feared fire – then the torch might be all he needed to complete his Quest. He headed deeper into the forest, eyes straining against the darkness. The trees threw shifting shadows on

the ground, so there seemed to be movements all around. Tom could feel the thump of his heart in his chest.

What if I'm too late?

He heard the Beast's foul hissing, and quickened his steps, following the sound. Then the torchlight flickered over the pale mass of Skurik's body. He found the Beast snapping and snorting at the sky as Elenna worked her way along a branch above, trying to reach the suspended children. Each coal-black eye tracked her movements.

"Try this!" said Tom, drawing his sword. He tossed it up, hilt first, and Elenna caught it. Skurik spun round, and a blast of his revolting breath washed over Tom.

"Won't you need it?" Elenna asked.

Tom held out the torch. "It's not steel that Skurik fears," he said.

The Beast snarled, lunging at Tom then dropping back. His body pulsed and glistened in the firelight, and his eyes narrowed. Tom waved the torch in front of him and almost caught Skurik's hide. The Beast shrieked and Tom saw a patch of foul skin blacken and bubble.

"No taste for flames, have you?" Tom taunted the Beast.

Skurik skirted in a wide circle around Tom, looking for an opening. But Tom kept the torch between them. The Forest Demon spurted a spray of gluey drool, and Tom lifted his shield just in time. The sludge splatted into the wood, and ripped the shield from his arm. He watched the tendrils suck it back into Skurik's gaping throat and swallow the shield whole. *I'm defenceless!*

Skurik lunged forward and sprayed Tom again. This time he leaped aside. His torch tangled in the undergrowth. *Oh no!* He heard the crackle of burning leaves and realised a patch of ferns had caught alight.

Tom stamped the flames down with his boots, bringing the torch around to ward Skurik off. In return, the Beast snapped his teeth a sword's length from Tom's face. The waft of foul breath made him stagger backwards.

Skurik's not stupid, thought Tom. *One wrong move and I'll be following my shield into his jaws.* He wondered how many other brave warriors had met their end in those jagged jaws, following the Warrior's Road. *This is why the Judge sent me here*, Tom thought. *To perish. Well, I shan't!*

Tom leaped up onto a tree stump. Above, he saw that Elenna was slicing through a sticky sac, pulling the first of the dazed children to safety. Skurik roared at the sky, and the children cried out with terror. He fired another jet of slime, and Tom had to somersault off to avoid it. He almost found himself trapped against a thicket, but slipped aside. *That was too close. I need to be more careful.*

He stumbled over a fallen splintered

branch and its sharp point gave him
a sudden idea. *Time to spike this giant
maggot…* As Skurik heaved his bulbous
form around to face him, Tom hooked
his toe beneath the branch, and
lowered the torch.

"Come and get me, slug face!"

Skurik's eyes sparkled with hatred

and he opened his mouth wide to deliver a barrage of drool. Tom flicked the branch into the air with his foot, then caught it with his sword hand. Using it like a spear, he launched the branch into the gaping jaws and the tip lodged in Skurik's throat.

The Beast heaved and gagged, his whole body shaking. But he couldn't dislodge the log. *I've got you now*, Tom thought. He brought the torch around and wafted it in Skurik's face. The Forest Demon, with a choking shriek, backed away into the tangled brambles of the thicket, smearing the ground with squelching slime.

Tom pushed on, pressing the torch close to Skurik's gleaming skin.

The Beast's eyes blinked in panic and fear, but he could go nowhere.

"Yield!" cried Tom.

CHAPTER TEN

THE JOURNEY CONTINUES

Skurik gave a snarl of rage, his head rising up. Tom followed it with the torch.

"Give up!" he said. "Or you will die."

Skurik's body flopped to the ground in defeat.

His eyes all closed at the same time, and his skin began to bubble. Tom stepped back as a stinking smoke rose from the Beast's bulbous body. The Forest Demon's flesh hissed and popped and melted like jelly, falling to pieces.

But it wasn't the fire melting him. The Beast was simply collapsing in front of Tom. Soon Skurik was no more than a foul puddle of slime at Tom's feet, soaking into the ground. Left behind was Tom's shield, and two balls of what looked like hardened sludge.

The Forest Demon was gone.

Back in the clearing, the slimy sacs that Elenna hadn't opened yet sank slowly to the ground, dangling from the gluey tendrils. Each sac landed softly on the forest floor, and the children inside began to claw their way out. They were covered in a thin white film, their clothes rotting away in patches, but otherwise they were unharmed. Elenna clambered down and offered Tom's sword back to him. He sheathed it gratefully.

"Is the monster dead?" asked a little girl. Her red hair was matted with slime.

For now, thought Tom, *until another warrior walks the Road.*

"It won't harm you again," said

Elenna. "Your parents are waiting. Get yourselves home."

"Follow me," said one of the older boys. "I know the way."

The children of Errinel ran from the clearing and back towards their village.

Tom was about to follow when the two strange lumps of solid sludge caught his eye again. They seemed to be changing shape, splitting into several parts like fingers.

"They're gloves!" he said, picking them up.

"Don't they smell?" asked Elenna, screwing up her face.

Tom shook his head. "The Beasts must each give up a token," he said. "Perhaps they'll be useful further along our journey."

They walked back out of the forest

as the moonlight seeped between the branches of the trees. At the forest's edge, they found the villagers gathering, hugging their children happily.

Lennard held out a hand to Tom. Kreg was hiding shyly behind his legs.

"We all owe you our deepest thanks," he said. "You are your father's son indeed. You and your brave friend must stay and enjoy our feast – a midnight one!"

Aunt Maria and Uncle Henry approached the group, with Silver bounding between them like a ghostly grey shadow. He pressed his nose into Elenna's hand.

"Yes, please stay, Tom," said his uncle. "Who better to be the guest of honour at our feast? We can make up your old bed."

"And I'll bake a cherry pie," said Aunt Maria.

Tom was about to agree. After such a hard battle, some food and a good night's rest was just what he needed. But in the corner of his eye a red glow appeared. The Warrior's Road was like a trail of embers leading back into the forest. "I'm afraid we cannot stay," he said. "A hard journey awaits us."

Aunt Maria's face fell, but she nodded.

Kreg peered out from behind his father. He was clutching a wooden sword.

"You're the Master of the Beasts, aren't you?" he asked. "I want to be Master of the Beasts one day!"

The boy swished his sword clumsily, and Lennard cried "Ouch!" as it hit

him on the shin.

Tom grinned at the young boy.
"Then keep practising with that
sword. Next time I pass through, we'll
have a duel."

He and Elenna said goodbye to
the villagers, and started to walk
away. Tom followed the red track
that only he could see. It led back

to the clearing, but where Skurik had disappeared there now stood an archway of dripping resin, glistening silver. Tom sucked in a breath.

"Stay close," he said. "I think the Warrior's Road might be taking us to another kingdom altogether."

Elenna laid a hand on his shoulder. "I suppose I'd better trust you!"

Tom led her towards the arch, and a strange, light feeling spread across his skin, making the fine hairs on the back of his neck stand up. Silver whined uneasily.

"Ready?" he asked Elenna.

"As I'll ever be," she said.

Five more Beasts to face, and any one of them could take their lives. Tom thought back to the boy Kreg's question. *You're Tom, aren't you, Master of the Beasts?*

I was once, he thought, stepping under the arch. *And while there's blood in my veins, I will be again.*

Join Tom on the next stage
of the Beast Quest, when he faces

TARGRO
THE ARCTIC MENACE!

Series 13: THE WARRIOR'S ROAD
COLLECT THEM ALL!

The Warrior's Road is Tom's toughest challenge
yet. Will he succeed where so many have failed?

SKURIK
THE FOREST DEMON

978 1 40832 402 8

TARGRO
THE ICE MENACE

978 1 40832 403 5

SLIVKA
THE COLD-HEARTED CURSE

978 1 40832 404 2

LINKA
THE SKY CONQUEROR

978 1 40832 405 9

VERMOK
THE SPITEFUL SCAVENGER

978 1 40832 406 6

KOBA
GHOUL OF THE SHADOWS

978 1 40832 407 3

Win an exclusive
Beast Quest T-shirt and goody bag!

Tom has battled many fearsome Beasts and we want to know
which one is your favourite! Send us a drawing or painting of
your favourite Beast and tell us in 30 words why you think
it's the best.

Each month we will select **three** winners to receive
a Beast Quest T-shirt and goody bag!

Send your entry on a postcard to
BEAST QUEST COMPETITION
Orchard Books, 338 Euston Road, London NW1 3BH.

Australian readers should email:
childrens.books@hachette.com.au

New Zealand readers should write to:
Beast Quest Competition, 23 O'Connell St, Auckland 1010,
NZ, or email: childrensbooks@hachette.co.nz

**Don't forget to include your name and address.
Only one entry per child.**

Good luck!

Join the Quest,
Join the Tribe

www.beastquest.co.uk

Have you checked out the Beast Quest website?
It's the place to go for games, downloads, activities,
sneak previews and lots of fun!

You can read all about your favourite Beasts,
download free screensavers and desktop wallpapers
for your computer, and even challenge your friends
to a Beast Tournament.

Sign up to the newsletter at www.beastquest.co.uk
to receive exclusive extra content and the
opportunity to enter special members-only
competitions. We'll send you up-to-date info on all
the Beast Quest books, including the next exciting
series which features four brand-new Beasts!

Get 30% off all Beast Quest Books at www.beastquest.co.uk
Enter the code BEAST at the checkout.

LOOK OUT FOR SERIES 2:

THE CAVERN OF GHOSTS

OUT SEPTEMBER 2013

978 1 40832 411 0   978 1 40832 412 7   978 1 40832 413 4   978 1 40832 414 1

COMING SOON!

SPECIAL BUMPER EDITION

978 1 40831 6~~

www.seaquestbooks.co.uk